DANGER! ACTION! TROUBLE! ADVENTURE!

THE D.A.T.A. SET

Don't Disturb the Dinosaurs

WITHDRAWN

By Ada Hopper   Illustrated by Sam Ricks

LITTLE SIMON
New York London Toronto Sydney New Delhi

LITTLE SIMON

An imprint of Simon & Schuster Children's Publishing Division

1230 Avenue of the Americas, New York, New York 10020

First Little Simon hardcover edition April 2016

Copyright © 2016 by Simon & Schuster, Inc. All rights reserved, including the right of reproduction in whole or in part in any form. LITTLE SIMON is a registered trademark of Simon & Schuster, Inc., and associated colophon is a trademark of Simon & Schuster, Inc. For information about special discounts for bulk purchases, please contact Simon & Schuster Special Sales at 1-866-506-1949 or business@simonandschuster.com. The Simon & Schuster Speakers Bureau can bring authors to your live event. For more information or to book an event contact the Simon & Schuster Speakers Bureau at 1-866-248-3049 or visit our website at www.simonspeakers.com.

Designed by John Daly. The text of this book was set in Serifa.

Manufactured in the United States of America 0216 FFG 10 9 8 7 6 5 4 3 2 1

Library of Congress Cataloging-in-Publication Data

Hopper, Ada. Don't disturb the dinosaurs / by Ada Hopper ; illustrated by Sam Ricks. — First Little Simon paperback edition. pages cm. — (The DATA Set ; #2) Summary: Thanks to Dr. Bunsen's latest wacky invention, second-graders Gabriel, Laura, and Cesar, aka the DATA Set, are blasted back to the prehistoric era, where they quickly find themselves dashing from flying pterosaurs, stomping stegosaurus stampedes, and a sharp-toothed T. rex.

ISBN 978-1-4814-5731-6 (pbk) — ISBN 978-1-4814-5732-3 (hardback) — ISBN 978-1-4814-5733-0 (eBook) [1. Time travel—Fiction. 2. Dinosaurs—Fiction. 3. Clubs—Fiction. 4. Adventure and adventurers—Fiction.] I. Ricks, Sam, illustrator. II. Title. III. Title: Do not disturb the dinosaurs. PZ7.1.H66Do 2016 [Fic]—dc23 2015018119

CONTENTS

Chapter 1

Blast to the Past

Fwoosh. A hot breeze rustled through the jungle tree leaves.

Screech! A wild animal's cry echoed in the distance.

Rummmmmble.

"What was that?" Laura Reyes whispered nervously.

"That was my stomach," said

Cesar Garcia. "I should have eaten a bigger breakfast."

The friends rolled their eyes. But another wild animal cry rang out, and Laura, Cesar, Gabriel Martinez, and Stego the Stegosaurus huddled closer together.

"Guys," said Gabriel, "I do not think we are in Newtonburg anymore."

Gabe was definitely right. These three whiz kids, known as the DATA Set, were indeed no longer in their home town of Newtonburg. The question was, where were they?

"Okay, let's retrace

our steps from the beginning," said Laura. "Dr. B.'s growth ray accidentally brought our toy animals to life."

"Then they started growing," continued Cesar.

"And we had to sneak them into the zoo," remembered Gabe. "Except for Stego."

"Yeah," Cesar chimed in. "Dr. B. was going to use his time machine to send Stego back in time."

"Then what happened?" Laura asked. "Where are we?"

"Dr. B. happened," Gabe said. "I'll bet his time machine must have malfunctioned just like the growth ray did. He accidentally sent us to a rain forest."

"I've read lots of books on rain forests," said Cesar. "And none of them had one of those. . . ."

He pointed overhead.

Soaring high above them was an enormous creature with a brightly colored head crest. It had leathery wings that stretched wide and a narrow, razor-sharp beak.

"Please tell me that's a bird," Laura said in disbelief.

"Not unless it was hit by Dr. Bunsen's growth ray too," said Cesar. "There aren't any birds that large that can fly."

"It's not a bird," Gabriel said. His eyes suddenly shone brightly, and a huge grin crossed his face.

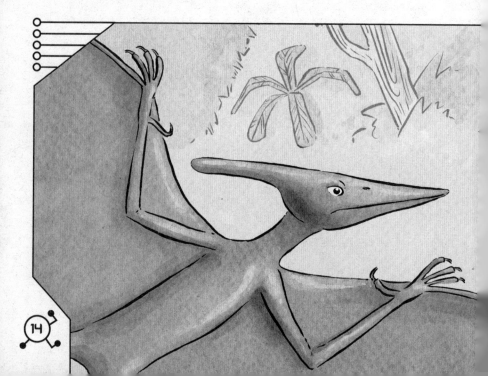

"It's a *Pterosaur*!"

"A what?" Laura asked.

"Dr. B.'s invention worked." Gabe breathed. "He sent us back with Stego to the Jurassic period. DATA Set . . . we're in the time of the dinosaurs!"

Chapter 2

A Jurassic Mistake

Meanwhile, back in present-day Newtonburg, Dr. Gustav Bunsen was very worried.

"DATA Set?" he called.

But Gabriel, Laura, and Cesar were nowhere to be seen.

"Oh, dear . . ."

Admittedly, he had forgotten to

warn the three friends to stand back when he activated his time-travel machine. But surely he hadn't . . .

"They must be hiding," the doctor assured himself. "Very clever, my young friends! An amusing prank. You can come out now!"

Dr. Bunsen looked behind his molecular generator. No Gabriel. He

checked underneath his UFO detector. No Laura. He opened the double doors of his oversize pantry. All the food was still there. No Cesar.

"Well, then, there's only one explanation," the doctor declared. "They have been sent along with Stego back to the prehistoric era. On the one hand, it's quite exciting. My invention worked! On the other hand, I've almost certainly doomed them to a dinosaur-dinner fate. . . ."

The doctor looked at his machine. "But what I have sent back in time, I can bring home again! I just need to reverse the polarization . . . and reset the time continuum frequency . . . and *huzzah*!"

The doctor pressed the control button, expecting the same bright green flash as before, which would

bring the DATA Set home.

Beep. Boop. Bvzhoooooomm . . .

His time machine shut down.

"Oh. Well. Now, that *is* the worst time for a time machine to break."

Suddenly, the front doorbell rang.

"Of course!" Dr. Bunsen cried. "I must have sent the children back in time a few minutes. They are at my door now. I have *not* messed up in a Jurassic way!"

Dr. Bunsen took the basement laboratory steps two at a time as he

raced to the front door. He flung it wide open . . .

. . . and outside was a child with an incredibly small head!

"Ahhh!" screamed the doctor.

"WAHHH!" cried the child.

"Dr. Bunsen?" It was Mrs. Martinez, holding Gabe's little sister. She smiled politely. "I'm Gabriel's mother, and this is Juanita, his baby sister."

"Ah, yes," the worried doctor mumbled to himself. "A little baby. That does make more sense than a grown-up with a very tiny head."

"Yes, well, I am looking for Gabriel," said Mrs. Martinez. "Have you seen him? Is he here?"

"I see." The doctor nervously adjusted his goggles on his head.

"I'm afraid he's not here. At least, not at this moment. In time."

Gabe's mother shook her head with a confused smile. "Gabe mentioned that you have a silly way of saying things. Well, as long as they're playing safely, just let Gabe know to be home in time for dinner.

I have a special treat for him."

"The operative word there being 'safely,' as it were." The doctor rubbed the back of his neck. "Well, I shall certainly let him know to be home. In time. For dinner."

Gabe's mother laughed, a bit bewildered, before she turned down the walkway.

Dr. Bunsen, however, was start-
ing to grow more worried than
excited.

How could he have the DATA Set home in time for dinner when he wasn't even sure *where in time* they were?

Chapter 3

Walking with Dinos

"I cannot believe this!" Gabe exclaimed as the friends walked through the jungle. "We're seeing real live dinosaurs. This is so cool!"

"You may think it's cool," said Laura. "But I don't want to become a dino's lunch!"

"Me neither," added Cesar.

"Relax, guys," Gabe said with a confident grin. "I know everything there is to know about dinosaurs. I'll make sure we stay clear of the dangerous ones. No sweat."

It was true. Gabe was fascinated by dinosaurs. He knew which

era each one lived in, what they liked to eat, and even which dinosaurs were *not* actually dinosaurs. (Correcting his science teacher when she referred to a prehistoric reptile as a "dinosaur" was one of Gabe's favorite challenges.)

"But how are we going to get home?" Laura insisted. "Where will we stay?"

"What will we *eat*?" asked Cesar, suddenly alarmed. "I am not surviving on prehistoric bugs!"

"Don't worry," Gabe replied

with a ridiculously wide smile still plastered on his face. "I'm sure Dr. B. will find us. Maybe he even meant to send us back, so we could help Stego find a nice herd of Stegosauruses to live with."

Gabe patted the once-mini Stegosaurus affectionately on the nose. The effects of Dr. Bunsen's growth ray were still working on the tiny dinosaur. It would take a few more days before he reached his full size.

"Maybe," Laura said slowly. "But I hope Dr. B. doesn't take too long."

"We'll be fine," Gabe assured
her. "I'll be your dino-guide! I know
which ones are carnivores and eat
meat—we'll steer clear of those. I
know which ones are herbivores
and eat plants—we'll probably still

steer clear of those. And I know which ones—"

As Gabe was speaking, the giant Pterosaur from earlier suddenly swooped down, snatched up Stego, and flew off!

"STEGO!" the friends screamed.

"I'm guessing that dinosaur is a carnivore?" Cesar cried as they chased after it.

"Pterosaurs are technically flying reptiles," Gabe shouted. "But I thought they only ate fish! At least, that's what scientists say."

"Maybe they got it wrong," Laura said, leaping over a puddle of prehistoric goo.

The friends ran as fast as they could, but soon the Pterosaur was out of sight.

"We have to save Stego." Gabe
panted, holding his side.

Just then the ground shook with
several stomps.

The friends turned. An giant-size dinosaur was stalking toward them.

"Gabe, please tell me *that's* an herbivore," Cesar said.

Gabe shook his head. "That's definitely a carnivore . . . and it spotted us! Run!"

Chapter 4

Close Escape!

"I used to think T. rexes were cool!" Laura cried as the friends bounded through the jungle.

"That's not a T. rex," Gabe shouted back. "It's an Allosaurus. T. rexes won't appear until the late Cretaceous period. That's, like, ninety million years from now."

"Whatever it is, it would be cooler if it wasn't trying to eat us!" Cesar yelled.

The friends ran as fast as they could, but the huge dinosaur was gaining on them.

"We can't outrun it!" Laura realized.

"I have an idea," Gabe shouted. "Run in a zigzag.

We can confuse it!"

Quickly, the friends began zipping in and out of the thick jungle trees. The Allosaurus could not run through the tight spaces of the forest as easily as the kids. It roared in frustration.

"It's working!" exclaimed Gabe. "Climb up one of these trees while we have a head start!"

The friends leaped onto the low limbs of the nearest tree and began to shimmy up. But the trunk was slick. Cesar slipped!

"Catch!" Laura cried.

She tossed him a piece
of vine. Cesar gripped
it tight, and Gabe and Laura
hoisted him up just as the
Allosaurus reached them.
It chomped wildly, barely
missing Cesar's sneaker.

"Whoa!" Cesar yelled, yanking his foot up. "That was really close!"

"Keep on climbing," instructed Gabe. "If it can't see us, it will think it's lost us."

The three friends climbed up, up, up.

Down below, the Allosaurus roared and banged against the tree trunk. But soon the kids were out of sight. After a while, the dinosaur stopped roaring. It circled a few times, confused. Then another animal cry rang out in the jungle. Eagerly, the Allosaurus stalked off in search of an easier meal.

"Phew." Cesar sighed. "Thanks, guys." He looked at his sneaker. It was covered in Allosaurus saliva. "*Ewwwww.* Dino drool!"

"We still need to save Stego," Gabe reminded them.

"Gabe, do you really think we can find him?" Laura's face grew serious. "I mean, by now wouldn't the Pterosaur have . . . ?"

Gabe shook his head. "No. I'm telling you, Pterosaurs eat fish. Not dinosaurs."

"Maybe it didn't want to eat him," Cesar offered optimistically. "Maybe it wanted to protect Stego from the Allosaurus."

"Yeah, that must be it!" Gabe added hopefully. "It must have wanted to protect Stego from the Allosaurus. All we need to do is find the Pterosaur's nest, and we'll find Stego!"

Laura looked doubtful. "Gabe, I'm not sure . . ."

"That's what we're doing," Gabe said firmly. "The DATA Set doesn't leave one of our own behind."

"Okay," said Cesar. "Let's just steer clear of the carnivores from now on."

"Good idea," said Gabe. "Maybe we can see the Pterosaur's nest

from the top of this tree."

The friends began to shimmy even higher. Laura reached the tallest branch first. She pushed back the leaves and gasped.

"Can you see the Pterosaur's nest?" Gabe asked eagerly.

"Not exactly . . . ," whispered Laura. "Guys, we have another little problem."

Staring straight back at them was a dinosaur with a neck as tall as the tree they had just climbed. And this time, there was no escape!

Chapter 5

Operation: Rescue Stego

The dinosaur stared at the DATA Set. The DATA Set stared at the dinosaur.

Then it lowered its head toward Cesar, mouth open wide.

"Why does everything here want to eat *me*!" Cesar cried.

CHOMP! The dino took a huge

bite . . . right out of the branch next to Cesar.

"It's okay," said Gabe. "That's a Diplodocus. It only eats plants."

Cesar sighed. "Can we please establish which dinosaurs eat meat and which eat plants before I have a heart attack?"

The enormous dinosaur munched the branch slowly, staring at the kids. Then it plodded away, stretching its long neck out to take bites from the treetops as it went.

"Okay," said Gabe. "Now let's look for the Pterosaur's nest."

The friends pushed back the oversize leaves from the top of the tree and gazed out over the landscape. What they saw took their breath away.

The valley was filled with all

kinds of dinosaurs as far as they could see!

"I don't believe this," said Gabe.

"It's incredible," said Laura.

"It's the Pterosaur!" cried Cesar. He pointed. Not far away was a large outcropping of rocks. Circling a cliff high up was the Pterosaur!

"Good job, Cesar!" Gabe said. "That's where the nest is. And that's where we'll find Stego."

"How can we sneak past the dinosaurs down there?" Laura asked.

"We'll find a way," Gabe insisted. "Don't worry, Stego. We're coming for you!"

Gabe looked confident. But Laura could tell that he was really worried about his Stegosaurus friend. The thing was, Stego wasn't the only one in danger. In fact, Laura was pretty sure *they* were also in danger.

"I hope Dr. B. is coming for us," Laura said. "And I really hope his time machine isn't broken."

"Well, it's broken," declared the doctor.

Dr. Bunsen wheeled out from underneath his time machine, covered in oil.

"Apparently, these unbreakable

motor gears do, in fact, break." He
tossed the busted gears across the
lab with a loud clatter.

"We'll just need a new set of
gears. It's off to the store for me!"

The doctor grabbed his wallet
and bounded out of the laboratory.

Chapter 6

Don't Disturb the Dinos

"Remind me to bring supersize bug spray the next time we go on a Dr. B. adventure." Cesar swatted at the Jurassic-size insects hovering around him. The friends were cautiously making their way across the overgrown valley.

"Careful, Cesar," warned Laura.

"We don't know how pre-historic bugs will react. For all you know, they'll try to eat you too."

"I *would* leave them alone." Cesar ducked an enormous moth-type creature. "But they won't leave *me* alone!"

"They've never seen a human before," teased Gabe. "Maybe they're curious."

Laura suddenly stopped. "I didn't think about that," she said slowly. "We're not supposed to be here. So wouldn't anything we do technically . . . ?"

". . . alter the future?" Gabe finished for her just as Cesar whacked a flying insect on the tail. It buzzed away, dazed and angry.

"Cesar!" cried Gabe and Laura.

"What?" Cesar shrugged. "It's one bug!"

"We can't take any chances," Gabe said. "From now on, no more disturbing anything prehistoric."

"You mean, 'Don't Disturb the Dinos'?" Cesar joked.

"Exactly," said Gabe.

"Okay . . ." Laura shot Gabe a look. "So, we *shouldn't* raid a Pterosaur's nest, take back Stego, and bring him to live with a herd of full-size Stegosauruses?"

Gabe frowned. "That's different. We came here to give Stego a new home. We can't just leave him."

"I'm not saying we should leave him," said Laura, getting a little frustrated. "Just that we have to be careful. Anything we do could change the course of history. Including getting eaten by a dinosaur."

Gabe was quiet for a moment. "I know," he said finally. "But it's my fault he's in trouble. I'm the one who let him get hit by the growth ray. And I'm the

one who didn't protect him from the Pterosaur."

Laura felt bad for being hard on Gabe. "It's not your fault," she said more calmly. "How could you have known what scientists didn't even know?"

"Yeah," added Cesar. "And we're going to save him. Like you

said, we're the DATA Set. Danger is in our name."

Gabe looked at his friends gratefully. "Thanks, guys. I'm glad we're a team. Okay, so it's settled. 'Don't Disturb the Dinos.' Except for getting Stego to a herd of Stegosauruses to live with. But everything else is off-limits."

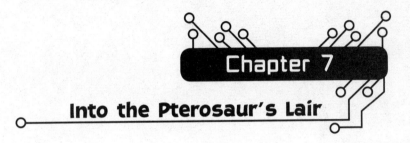

Chapter 7

Into the Pterosaur's Lair

Far across the valley, the DATA Set stood at the base of the rock face. It hadn't been easy getting there. They'd snuck around a group of Brachiosaurs, and they'd run for cover when a quick-footed Dryosaurus nearly spotted them. Gabe was 99.9 percent sure it

was an herbivore, but no one really wanted to stick around to find out. They'd even passed by a peaceful herd of Stegosauruses: the perfect family for Stego!

But now they faced their latest challenge: sneaking into the Pterosaur's lair.

"Remember the plan," Gabe said.

"When we get to the top, we wait until the Pterosaur flies away. Then we grab Stego and get out."

"Got it," replied Laura and Cesar.

Stealthily, the friends climbed up the rock face.

"Where's the Pterosaur?" Cesar asked when they reached the top.

"I don't know," Gabe said. "Maybe

it already left?"

THWOOP! THWOOP! THWOOP! THWOOP!

The friends dove behind a rock just as the Pterosaur swooped from the cave. It flew down, gliding deep into the valley.

"Now's our chance!" urged Gabe.

The friends raced inside the dark cavern.

The Pterosaur's nest was surrounded by leaves, branches, and small bones. Suddenly, something moved at the back of the cave. . . . "Stego!" Gabe cried.

The friends rushed forward and embraced the little dinosaur. He was safe and sound!

"I knew you hadn't been eaten, buddy," Gabe said, his voice breaking with relief. "I just knew it."

"You were right." Laura smiled happily. "Quick, let's get out of here before the Pterosaur comes back."

The friends tried to leave, but Stego wouldn't follow.

"Come on, buddy." Gabe tugged at the little dino's tail. "Time to go!"

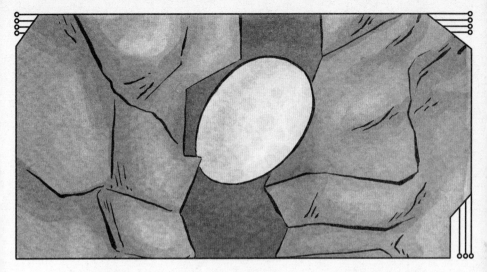

But Stego remained stubborn. He
grunted, nosing a crack in the cave
wall.

"He's trying to tell us something,"
said Gabe. He went over and peered
through the crack. Something round
was wedged inside the cave wall.

"It's an egg!" Gabe exclaimed. "A
Pterosaur egg! It must have rolled

in here and gotten stuck." Gabe glanced toward the creature's nest. "The Pterosaur must have thought the egg was stolen. Or . . . that it hatched. *That's* why the Pterosaur grabbed Stego! It thought he was its baby! It's a mother Pterosaur!"

"That means we *really* need to go," Laura insisted. "If it's a mother Pterosaur, she's going to be super-mad if she thinks we're taking her baby."

"But we can't just leave the egg trapped," said Gabe. "Quick. Can you put together some sort of lasso or stick to reach it?"

That definitely got Laura's attention. Inventions were her specialty, especially inventions using whatever materials happened to be lying around.

Moving lightning fast, Laura grabbed large, hollow reeds and vine bits from around the Pterosaur's nest. In no time at all, she had built a stick with a vine loop attached to the end that could reach well inside the crack.

Together, the friends used
the lasso stick to carefully maneuver
the Pterosaur egg out. They gently
placed it back inside the nest.

"Mission accomplished," said
Gabe.

"Let's get out of here," said Cesar. "I have a feeling our time is almost—"

THWOOP! THWOOP!

The Pterosaur had returned. It screeched furiously.

"—up," finished Cesar.

Chapter 8

Prehistoric Showdown

The Pterosaur snapped its long beak savagely at the DATA Set.

"Uh . . . I know they only eat fish," said Cesar. "But she looks pretty hungry."

"What do we do?" Laura asked.

Gabe had gone pale. "I don't know. We're trapped."

The Pterosaur came closer. There
was nothing separating it from the
DATA Set!

Suddenly, Stego moved between
the friends and the angry creature.

"Stego, no!" exclaimed Gabe.

The tiny Stegosaurus grunted and
let out dinosaur roars that sounded
like barking. Now the Pterosaur was

confused. It was unsure what to do
with its "baby" blocking it from the
intruders.

"He's protecting us!" cried Cesar.
"Way to go, Stego!"

Just then, a loud *craaaaaaaaack*
got everyone's attention.

Inside the nest, the Pterosaur egg
was rolling and breaking.

"It's hatching!" exclaimed Laura.

Distracted, the Pterosaur watched as its egg hatched, revealing a small, screechy, and very slimy baby Pterosaur!

"Incredible," breathed Gabe.

"Awesome!" said Laura.

"Our ticket out!" cried Cesar. "Come on!"

While the Pterosaur was distracted, the friends and Stego escaped.

They half climbed, half slid down the mountain. Before they knew it, they were on the ground.

"We did it, DATA Set!" Gabe beamed and gave Stego a big hug. "We saved you, buddy. Now let's find you a new home."

As the sun sank low on the horizon, the DATA Set and Stego hid in a thick bramble of bushes. The Stegosaurus herd was not far away.

"There they are, buddy," said Gabe. "You ready?"

The little dino grunted, staring intently out at the herd.

Gabe patted Stego's nose. "I'm going to miss you. Thanks for saving us. And for being such a great friend."

Stego's gaze shifted to Gabe while he continued to pet him.

"I wish I knew if he understood us," Gabe said a bit sadly.

Suddenly, Stego gave Gabe a great big lick! Then, before the kids could react, the happy little dino bounded out of the bushes toward the herd. When he reached them, the adult Stegosauruses looked at him for a long while. Slowly, three moved forward. They protectively

surrounded the little dinosaur, and one guided Stego into the center of the pack with its tail. Together, the herd moved off toward the setting sun.

Laura placed a hand on Gabe's shoulder. "He understood."

Chapter 9

Nightfall

A few hours later the DATA Set sat huddled in a jungle clearing. With night setting in and still no sign of Dr. Bunsen, the kids needed to find shelter until morning.

Laura built a tent out of sturdy tree limbs and leaves while Cesar hunched over a small pit filled with dry twigs. He rubbed two sticks together, trying to get a fire going.

Meanwhile, Gabe wrapped his arms around himself and gazed up at the night sky. Millions of stars twinkled—more brightly than he'd ever seen at home. Gabe wondered how many of them were still shining back in present-day Newtonburg and how many had burned out millions of years earlier.

"It's amazing," he said. He looked out over the horizon to where a cluster of volcanoes glowed red with smoldering lava. Shadows of giant flying creatures appeared and vanished among the peaks. It was all so incredible. And scary.

"I wonder what they're doing at home," he said.

"Me too," said Laura. "Do you think Dr. B. will come soon?"

"He'd better," piped up Cesar. "It's pizza night at my house. I haven't eaten all day! When we get home,

you guys can have a

slice."

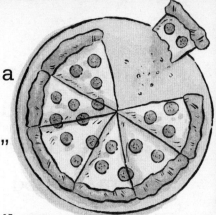

"If we get home,"
Gabe said quietly.

The friends fell silent.
None of them knew what would
happen if Dr. Bunsen didn't come
for them.

"I'm sorry I put us in danger
before," Gabe said. "I was so
excited to see real dinosaurs and
then worried about Stego. I didn't
think—"

"It's okay," Laura interrupted
him. "We're a team. We stick

together. No matter what."

Gabe smiled at Laura appreciatively, and she smiled back. Then Laura turned to Cesar. "How's the fire going?"

"Almost . . . got . . . it . . ." Cesar was rubbing the two sticks together. Suddenly, a tiny spark caught on the dried twigs. It ignited!

"I did it, guys!" Cesar cried. He jumped up and did a silly little dance.

The flickering light from the fire quickly illuminated the entire clearing. Suddenly, Gabe's and Laura's eyes grew wide.

"Cesar," Laura hissed. She motioned for him to come toward them.

Cesar stopped dancing. "There's
something really scary behind me,
isn't there?"

He turned. . . .

The Allosaurus from before was
there! It opened its mouth and let
out a huge *ROOOOOAR*, ready to
chomp Cesar!

"Oh no. Not this time!" Cesar grabbed a fiery stick from the pit and waved it at the dinosaur. *"Huzzah!"* he cried, just like the doctor.

A spark jumped and struck the Allosaurus on the nose! Scorched, the dinosaur howled. It took a few steps back before thundering off into the jungle, frightened away.

"Did you see that?" Cesar cried in disbelief. "Please tell me you saw that!"

"I most certainly did!" a voice cheered through the darkness.

The friends couldn't believe
their ears. Dr. Bunsen was stand-
ing at the edge of the clearing,

holding the remote control for his once-again-operational time machine. They were saved!

Chapter 10

Not So Far Away

Dr. Bunsen had returned the children home in time for dinner. Once the three friends and the doctor had blasted back to the present day, they'd told him all about their prehistoric adventure. The doctor was delighted that their mission had been a success! But he also realized how dangerous his time machine could be. The doctor had removed the motor gears from the machine on the spot, so it would never accidently transport someone again.

Then Dr. Bunsen had turned to Gabriel. "By the way, your mother stopped by. She said something about a 'special surprise.' I believe you'll want to hurry home."

"Mom, I'm home!" Gabe had never been happier to open his own front door. He was back, and it was dinnertime at the Martinez household.

Now Gabe stood in his family's kitchen. Juanita bounced in her high chair. His father sat at the table, working on his laptop. And his mother was by the sink.

Everything was back to normal. Just as it should be.

"There you are, *mi hijo*," Gabe's mom said. "Did you have fun today?"

Gabe smiled. "You have no idea."

"Well, I have a special surprise for you." Gabe's mom picked up an envelope and handed it to him. "Open it, sweetie!"

Gabe tore open the envelope and pulled out . . . three tickets to the Newtonburg Museum's dino exhibit.

"I know how much you love dinosaurs." Gabe's mother pinched his cheek. "I thought you might like to go with your friends."

Gabe wasn't sure if he should laugh or cry. He opted for an awkward smile instead. "Gee . . . umm, thanks, Mom. I can't wait to show Laura and Cesar. I'm sure they'll think it's . . . dino-tastic."

Later that night, in his pajamas and ready for bed, Gabe lined up his plastic dinosaur figurines on the windowsill. He had a T. rex, a Triceratops, and even an Allosaurus. But no Stego.

"I hope you're having fun, buddy, wherever you are."

He looked out the window and up at the night sky. The stars were shining brightly overhead. They may not have been shining as brightly as in the Jurassic period, but they were shining all the same.

Maybe Stego was even looking at the same stars, millions of years in the past.

Who knows? Gabe thought with a smile. *He could be thinking about me, too.*

Of course, there was no way of knowing. But some- how, realizing that the stars had existed through millions of years in the universe made Gabe feel like his dinosaur pal wasn't so far away after all.

CHECK OUT THE NEXT DATA SET ADVENTURE!

It was a bright and early Monday morning in Newtonburg. The sun was shining. The birds were chirping. Rush-hour traffic was backing up. The start to a perfectly ordinary day.

Except it wasn't.

"Where in the world is Laura?"

Gabe and Cesar pedaled their bikes at top speed. "We're going to be late!"

They ditched their bikes in Gabe's parents' driveway and raced to the backyard. Normally, the three friends known as the DATA Set (Danger! Action! Trouble! Adventure!) would already be on their way to school. But Laura hadn't shown up at the corner as usual.

Something was up.

THE DATA SET
FOR MORE DANGER! ACTION!
TROUBLE! ADVENTURE!
Visit thedatasetbooks.com
Little Simon